POWER CHARGED

A COLLECTION OF CHRISTIAN SHORT STORIES FOR CHILDREN

Written by
Norma Armand

POWER CHARGED

A COLLECTION OF CHRISTIAN SHORT STORIES FOR CHILDREN

ISBN 978-0-9559573-1-4

First Published 2015

Printed in Great Britain

DEDICATION

This collection of short stories is dedicated to
everyone who wants to see young people grow up
knowing Jesus Christ as their Lord and Saviour.

Norma Armand

ACKNOWLEGEMENT

I would like to acknowledge Liz Piper of St Luke's Church, Cranham, who inspired me to write these stories.

Norma Armand

Contents

PERSEVERANCE

Nine year old Ella stopped looking at her maths homework and gazed out of the window as Allegro, her cat, whizzed across the lawn like a black streak and vanished into the bushes. She envied him. He didn't have to worry about 'stupid maths.' She put her pen down, got up from the table and went outside.

It was warm and sunny in the garden and Ella rocked on her creaky swing and stared up at the blue sky and small white clouds that drifted slowly by.

"Ella!" mum called from the kitchen door. "Aren't you supposed to be doing your maths homework?"

"I'll do it later, mum," Ella replied, in full flight.

"It's best to get it over with. Then you can relax," mum said as she approached Ella.

"I can't do it anyway. It's too hard," Ella confessed unhappily.

"Then why don't we look at it together and see what the problem is?"

"Oh, do we have to?" Ella pleaded, as Allegro emerged empty mouthed and restless.

"Yes, we do," mum replied firmly.

At the table, Ella showed mum the information booklet she had been given. It showed how to work out the various maths problems she had been set.

"Hmm." Mum rubbed her chin. "I must admit this is not how I learnt maths when I was at school. It's very different. But I don't want to confuse you, so let's stick to how the school wants you to learn it."

"I hate maths," Ella moaned.

"You have to leave your feelings out of it, Ella, as hard as that may be. Being negative only prevents you from learning and understanding. You've got to be positive and believe that with God's help, you can do it. Just keep on trying until you succeed."

"I don't think it'll work."

"It will. I promise you. Do you remember when you were learning how to swim? It didn't seem possible at first, did it?"

Ella agreed. She was six and her brother Daniel, eight, when they went on holiday abroad. Their hotel had a shallow indoor pool, which was quieter than the outdoor ones. Ella didn't like water and feared drowning, unlike Daniel, who roared before leaping in with an almighty crash.

Mum encouraged her to sit on the edge and slosh her feet about before climbing in. The water came up to her neck and she screamed as a gigantic wave washed over her face and charged down her throat, thanks to Daniel's clowning. Mum gave him

3

a good telling off as Ella spluttered and coughed uncontrollably.

"I want to get out," Ella cried, her eyes stinging.

"Don't worry. You'll be all right," mum reassured her. "You'll soon get used to getting your face wet."

But Ella was not happy, so mum prayed she would not be afraid of the water and trust God to keep her safe.

Gradually, Ella began to calm down and mum taught her how to move her arms and legs. She was given a 'Noodle,' to wrap around her body and Ella soon grew accustomed to the water and swam about happily. Within days she felt ready to try a few strokes without the support of the 'Noodle,' and found herself moving further and further away from the edge, without sinking. Feeling bolder, she attempted to swim the pool's width and succeeded, and by the end of the holiday, Ella was swimming lengths comfortably.

"What did it take for you to learn how to swim in the end?" mum asked her.

"I kept on trying?"

"That's right, and do you know what it's called when you keep on trying?" Ella shrugged her shoulders. "It's called perseverance. It means never giving up, even when it's difficult. Now what are the benefits of knowing how to swim?"

"It's good fun and it's good exercise."

"That's right and it's an important life skill as it could save your life or somebody else's one day. Maths is an important life skill too, but for different reasons. It helps you to think clearly, which will help you in other subjects; and open up many job opportunities for you in the future. So you can look at maths as a seed that will bring a harvest in the right season."

"I never thought about it like that before."

"That's hardly surprising. Before we get started, shall we pray?" Ella nodded, closed her eyes and put her hands together. "Dear Jesus," mum

5

began, "thank you for everything we have and everything you do for us. Please help Ella to understand maths and do the best she can. Thank you Lord, for hearing our prayer. Amen."

"Amen," Ella echoed.

"Now let's start working through these exercises," mum said and went through the various methods with Ella and wrote down additional examples.

"I'm going to leave you to get on with the rest of the questions and I'll come back and see how you're getting on in half an hour or so. And remember, if you get stuck at any time, keep praying and asking God to make it clear to you. Okay?"

"Yes, mum."

Ella swept away her negative thoughts and replaced them with positive ones instead. She felt God was helping her and understood why she needed to persevere and finished the remaining exercises without any problems.

"Well done," mum said after checking her daughter's answers. "You've got them all right. Do you still hate maths?"

"Well," Ella twisted her mouth, "not as much as I did before."

"That's the spirit, Ella." Mum gave her a big hug. "Keep up the good work. Now you can go outside and play."

"Thanks, mum."

Ella's face lit up as she ran into the garden and scooped up Allegro in her arms.

"I can do it," she told Allegro and laughed as the cat stared at her, wondering what all the fuss was about.

V.I.P

"Hello. Is that Mrs Peters?"

"Yes, it is."

"It's Miss Kenwood here."

"Hello, Miss Kenwood."

"I'm ringing up about Alex."

"What has he done this time?"

Hardly a week went by without a phone call from Miss Kenwood, deputy head of Alex's primary school.

"He's been disruptive in class, not listening to his teacher and has spent the last period with me. Can you come in and see me at three thirty?"

"Of course. I'll see you then."

"Thank you, Mrs Peters."

As Mrs Peters approached the school office, she felt as if she had been the naughty pupil and not her son, even though she knew this feeling of guilt was not from God.

Miss Kenwood led Mrs Peters into her office, where Alex sat with folded arms and a stony face.

Miss Kenwood gave her the details of Alex's behaviour, and then waited for a response from Alex, which did not come.

"Well, Alex," said Mrs Peters, "what have you got to say for yourself?"

"Sorry." Alex dragged the word through his lips.

"What are you sorry for?"

"For misbehaving in class and not doing as I was told," he recited without enthusiasm.

"And what are you going to do differently to stop this from happening in the future?"

"I'm going to do as I'm told," he said robotically.

"I'll have a good talk with him when we get home," Mrs Peters offered, hoping to end the meeting.

"As you know, Mrs Peters, we have been here before and there has been very little improvement. I'm of the opinion that Alex needs to have an assessment done so that this or another establishment can best meet your son's educational needs."

"I don't think that's necessary. There's nothing wrong with him. He's just a child. He'll grow out of it."

"Meanwhile, pupils in his class are having their education disrupted and teachers are unable to teach because of Alex."

Mrs Peters had to bite her lip to stop the tears from falling from her eyes as she ushered Alex home. She wasn't very fond of Miss Kenwood and didn't believe she had her son's best interests at heart. Alex had been brought up in a loving Christian home and knew right from wrong. She needed to get to the bottom of Alex's problems and fast.

"Alex," mum said after dinner. "We really need to sort this out. Why did you misbehave in class today?"

"Rory splashed my picture with paint, so I flicked some back and it ended up all over his shirt."

"What could you have done when Rory spoilt your picture?"

"Tell the teacher and I did, but she wouldn't listen to me. That's when I got angry and got into trouble."

"When did you tell the teacher?"

"After Rory told her what I'd done."

"It was too late by then. You should have told her straight away, instead of getting your own back first. You need to think carefully before you act. Ask yourself, 'Am I doing the right thing?' It won't always feel right, but it's what's best for you and pleasing to God. We're not responsible for other people's behaviour, but we are responsible for our own."

"Okay, mum. I'll try."

"Is there anything else bothering you, Alex?"

"No. The teachers just don't like me."

"The question is, Alex, do you like yourself?" Alex slowly shook his head.

"Why's that, love?"

"Because everybody's smarter than me."

"That's not true."

"Shelby's smarter than me."

"People are intelligent in different ways. Your sister may be a fast learner, but you're good at things she's not. You're more creative for instance."

"That doesn't count."

"Of course it does. God didn't make us all the same did he? That's why some people are doctors and others are musicians. Did you know that you're a V.I.P?"

"What's a V.I.P?"

"A very important person."

"That's silly. I'm not famous."

"You don't have to be," mum explained. "You're important because God says you are. Jesus was the most important person that lived on earth. He cared so much about you that he died on the cross so that you could live forever. He knows everything about you and is interested in everything you do. He has great plans for you and wants what's best for you, but you have to do things his way and that means following his commandments."

"I'm a V.I.P." Alex grinned and patted his chest.

"You are, Alex. So remember that when you're not feeling very smart. I want you to realise that you're not in competition with other people. You're in competition with yourself. So stop comparing yourself with other people. It's not about being the best, but being the best that you can be. Keep surprising yourself and then you'll feel a lot happier and more confident." She kissed the top of his head. "Why don't we say a prayer to God right now?" mum suggested, and Alex put his hands together and closed his eyes.

"Dear Lord, thank you that Alex is a very important person to you and that you are always with him. I pray that he will turn to you for divine guidance every day of his life and exceed all expectations in school and in every area of his life. I ask this in Jesus' mighty name. Amen."

"Amen," Alex said with a serene look on his face.

"Let's show Miss Kenwood that she's got you all wrong," mum said.

"Yeah. I'll show her," Alex added with determination.

That evening Alex drew a picture of himself with the initials V.I.P. written across the top and a symbol of the cross beside it.

"That's fantastic," mum praised him. "Let's put it on the wall so that you can see it every day."

From then on, Alex started concentrating in class and his work and behaviour steadily improved. Mrs Peters stopped receiving phone calls from Miss Kenwood, and the next time the deputy head contacted her, it was to praise Alex's miraculous transformation!

JEALOUSY

"Come on, Shannon, we're waiting for you!" mum called from the bottom of the stairs.

"I feel sick!" Shannon cried out.

"Oh no! Do you want to wait in the car while I go and see what the problem is?"

"Will do," Chris said.

Mum climbed the stairs and entered Shannon's room. She found her daughter lying on the bed clutching her stomach.

"What's wrong?" mum asked.

"I don't feel well."

"In what way?"

"My stomach hurts."

"What did you have for breakfast?"

"Cereal."

"So did I. You were okay five minutes ago. What else have you eaten?"

"Nothing."

Mum placed a hand on Shannon's forehead. It felt cool.

"Chris is waiting for us in the car. I'll go and get you a glass of water."

"Okay."

"Drink it all up," mum said on her return. Chris honked twice on his car horn. "We need to get going, Shannon, otherwise we'll hit traffic."

"Can't you leave me here?"

"Of course not, and it's too short notice for someone else to stay with you."

"Ooh," Shannon groaned.

"Is it really bad?" asked mum. Shannon nodded. "Okay. I'll have to tell Chris we're not going."

When Shannon heard Chris's car drive off, she smiled.

"How are you feeling?" mum asked her a little later.

"A bit better."

"Good. I'm glad about that, but I'm feeling a bit frustrated. I was really looking forward to the three of us going out together for the day."

"*We* can still do something, mum."

"I know, but it's not the same. I wanted you and Chris to get to know each other better."

"Why?"

"Because I care about him."

"I want you to care about me."

"I do darling, you must know that."

"I don't!"

"What's brought all this on? We spend loads of time together. Ever since your dad died three years ago it's always been just the two of us."

"And that's how I want it to stay. We don't need Chris."

Mum paused as she considered her response. "Don't you want me to have friends, Shannon?" Shannon didn't answer. "Is that the real reason you didn't want to go out today?"

"I don't want him to take you away from me," Shannon said, her voice trembling.

"Shannon, I won't let anyone ever do that. You're my number one priority. I want you to be happy more than anything else in the world."

"Then stop spending more time with him than with me."

"I don't think I do, but I'm not getting into an argument with you about it. I should have realised how you felt sooner."

"Does that mean you'll stop seeing him?"

"No it doesn't, Shannon."

"Why not?"

"Because there's enough room in my life for both of you."

"We'll see about that." Shannon narrowed her eyes.

"I hope you're not going to pull any more tricks, Shannon, because it won't work. Jealousy is a dangerous thing. The Bible says it's a cancer, which is an evil that quickly spreads until it takes you over. That's what happened in the story of Cain and Abel, Adam and Eve's sons. Cain was jealous of his brother because God accepted Abel's offering but rejected Cain's because it wasn't good enough. God warned him that sin was waiting to overtake him and to resist temptation. But he didn't listen. He led Abel into a field and killed him."

"I can't help the way I feel."

"You can actually. You can do it by changing the way you think about something or someone and in this case, Chris. You're looking at him as your enemy at the moment, instead of a friend. Why not try to find out what sort of person he is and the things he likes to do. Give him a fair chance. When you've done that, if you still don't like him, then I'll consider whether to continue seeing him. But I want you to be positive. I realise that I should have involved you in where we were going today and not just told you last night. So I want you to tell me where you'd like the three of us to go together."

"I don't know."

"Well, have a think about it."

The following weekend Shannon, mum and Chris went ice skating. Shannon moved confidently on the ice. Mum was slower and more cautious. Chris sat in the gallery watching them.

"Why doesn't Chris get on the ice?" Shannon asked mum, as they levelled with each other.

"Chris said he'd just watch for a bit," mum answered, staying close to the sides.

As they came up to Chris, mum asked him if he was coming on.

"I think I'll pass," Chris said.

"Come on, Chris. It's really easy. I'll teach you," Shannon said enthusiastically.

"Go on," mum urged him. "I'll sit and watch."

Chris reluctantly climbed onto the ice and gripped the rubber barrier.

"Just hold onto my hand and I'll take you round," Shannon said.

It took Chris several minutes before he was able to let go of the sides and take Shannon's hand.

"Don't worry. I'll go really slowly," Shannon said, as they moved off unsteadily. Chris started to wobble.

"When you feel like you're going to fall, just lean forward and you'll be fine."

Chris did the opposite. His legs flew up in the air and he landed on his bottom.

Shannon laughed as she helped him up.

"I think I've had enough," Chris said, winded.

"You're not giving up that easily. Let's get all the way around first."

Chris persevered, slipping once or twice, but managing to stay on his feet. Before long he could go around unsupported.

Afterwards they ate burgers and chips in the restaurant.

"Thanks for teaching me how to skate, Shannon. I've always had a fear of the ice," Chris admitted.

"That's okay," Shannon said.

"Yes, well done," mum added, with pride in her eyes.

"We'll have to go skating again," Shannon said.

"I think I need to recover from this experience first," Chris replied, rolling his eyes, which made Shannon laugh.

GREED

Martin kept his finger on the doorbell.

Dylan's mum rushed to the door and opened it.

"Hello again. What's up?"

Martin rushed in and entered the lounge.

"I've lost the money," he said.

"What money?"

"The deposit money."

"When did you last see it?"

"I definitely had it when I was here."

"So someone must've taken it when you left."

"It was zipped up in my inside pocket. There's no way someone got in there without me knowing about it."

"Could it have fallen out?"

"It's unlikely. That's why I thought I'd come back here and look," Martin said and began scouring the room.

Dylan's mum helped him look all over the flat, but neither could find the money.

"Dylan!" Mum entered her son's room, closely followed by Martin.

"Martin has lost some money from his jacket pocket. I don't suppose you've seen it anywhere?"

"Why would I?" Dylan answered, not looking up from his computer game.

"It's just that it's a lot of money and we really need to find it."

"Are you sure you haven't seen it?" Martin asked.

"Yes," Dylan replied.

"Did you take the money out of my jacket pocket?"

"Dylan wouldn't do that," mum answered for him.

"Well, *did* you?" Martin pressed.

"I don't know what you're talking about," Dylan replied.

"I'm talking about the money, Dylan. Where is it?" Martin persisted.

"He doesn't know," mum said.

"I'm not so sure about that," Martin said. "Look me in the eye, Dylan and tell me you didn't take it."

Dylan glanced up briefly and slid his eyes to one side. "I didn't take it."

"He's lying," Martin said.

"Dylan, if you have taken Martin's money, you'd better tell us now because I'm going to search every inch of this room."

Dylan looked from Martin to mum, blinking rapidly as his face started to crumble.

"Where is it?" Martin repeated.

"Under here," Dylan said and got off the bed.

Martin lifted the mattress and retrieved the roll of money.

"Is it all here?" Martin asked. Dylan nodded. "I'll count it anyway. Just to be sure."

"Dylan, how could you do such a thing?" mum asked.

Dylan shrugged his shoulders as he twisted his body from side to side.

"It's all here," Martin said after a while and looked wearily at Dylan. "What have you got to say for yourself?"

"Sorry," Dylan said, tears streaking down his cheeks.

"I'll let your mum have a word. I'd better get going," Martin said and pecked Dylan's mum on the cheek before leaving.

"Let's go to the kitchen. I think I need a cup of tea," mum said to Dylan.

27

Dylan followed her into the kitchen and slumped at the table.

"Why did you do it?" she asked after sipping her tea.

"I don't know."

"What were you going to do with the money?"

"Spend it."

"On what?"

"All kinds of things." Dylan's eyes lit up.

"Such as?"

"Designer clothes."

"So the clothes I buy you aren't good enough for you?"

"They're too cheap."

"I see. So you were going to buy these designer clothes and I wouldn't ask you where they came from?"

"I would have said dad bought them for me."

"Your dad doesn't have the money to buy you designer clothes. Have you asked him to?"

"He said he'd buy me something for Christmas."

"And you couldn't wait that long?"

"Why should I have to wait?"

"Because when you wait for something you really want, you appreciate it more."

"But you wouldn't buy me those new trainers I asked for."

"That's no excuse, Dylan. Don't try to shift the blame onto me. You stole the money and you knew it was the wrong thing to do. I haven't bought you up to do things like this. The Bible says that the love of money is the root of all evils. It causes people to do bad things and the consequences are that they end up losing everything. Worse than that is their separation from God.

Now I'm not saying there's anything wrong with having nice things, if you've worked hard and can afford them. But having lots of stuff doesn't make you happy because the more you have, the more you want. When people buy new things like clothes or trainers, they're excited about it at first, then after a while they get discarded for something else. It's the same with mobile phones. People always want an upgrade."

"What's wrong with that?"

"The point I'm making is that none of these things make us happy, even though the advertisers do a good job in making us believe they will. That's their job. What makes people truly happy is having a personal relationship with God, doing his will and caring about other people. You don't look convinced, but you'll understand this for yourself one day. Have you any idea what that money was for?"

"No."

"It was the deposit for your Go Karting party."

"I didn't know."

"That's something you really wanted for your birthday. We wanted to give you a surprise."

Dylan shook his head. "I've been really stupid, haven't I?"

"Not stupid, just misguided."

"I won't do anything like that ever again."

"I believe you, Dylan, but I think you should be saying that to God."

"Can you pray for me, mum?"

"I could, but I want you to ask God to forgive you and then you'll be able to put this sorry affair behind you."

"Okay, mum, I will." Dylan said, closed his eyes and put his hands together. "Dear God, I'm sorry I stole the money from Martin. Please forgive me. I promise not to steal anything ever again. Help me to be satisfied with the things I have and the things that mum can afford to buy me. Thank you that mum and Martin are going to let me have a Go Karting party, so that I can have fun with all my friends. Amen."

"Amen!"

FORGIVENESS

"How are you getting on with your invitations?" mum asked Madison, on entering her room.

"I'm nearly finished," Madison replied.

"Let me see," mum said and picked up the piece of paper to inspect the names.

"What's happened to Erin's name? I thought she'd be at the top of your list."

"I'm not inviting her," Madison said calmly.

"Why not? She's your closest friend."

"We're not friends any more. She's horrible."

"Why do you say that?"

"She didn't invite me to her birthday party."

"When was it?"

"Two weeks ago."

"And did she give you a reason?"

"When I asked, she said she'd run out of invitations, but I know it isn't true because she was acting funny with me before that. She's been going off with Bella and Emily at break times and when I've asked to go with them, she said I couldn't. And they've been saying horrible things about me behind my back, because they're always whispering and laughing when I'm around. I only found out about the party when Taiwo asked me if I was going."

"You must have felt awful."

"I don't really care anymore. I've got new friends now."

"I'm glad you make friends easily, Madison, but do you know why Erin turned against you?"

"We had a big argument and started calling each other names."

"I see."

"I know I shouldn't have, but she's so annoying at times."

"You can still invite her to your party."

"I don't want to."

"I know you don't, but it's the right thing to do."

"But I don't like her any more, mum."

"The fact that she didn't invite you to her party doesn't mean you shouldn't invite her to yours. It's important that you forgive Erin for the way she's behaved. Girls of your age are always falling out with each other. Besides, you could be friends again next week."

"I don't think so."

"Even so, I want you to invite her to your party."

"What if she doesn't want to come?"

"That's up to her. It's what *you* do that's important. Remember Jesus came to earth and forgave us for all the things we did wrong. He suffered and died on the cross for us and promised to forget about our bad behaviour because he loved us so much. So we have to learn to forgive other people, even if they have been unkind to us. When we don't, we only hurt ourselves.

There's a character in the Bible who forgave his brothers after they tried to kill him. Do you remember who that was?"

"Was it Joseph?"

"That's right. Joseph's brothers were so jealous of him that they threw him in a pit to die. Then they changed their minds and sold him into slavery instead. He was put in prison for something he didn't do, yet he ended up becoming second in command to the Pharaoh. When his brothers came to Egypt during the famine, he could have kept them all in jail or even had them killed for what they had done to him, but he didn't. He forgave them and treated them well."

"Okay," Madison sighed. "I'll invite her, but she probably won't come anyway."

"But she might," mum said optimistically.

The next day at school, Madison handed out her party invitations. However when she saw Erin, she could not bring herself to talk to her. She considered placing the invitation on her desk or giving it to someone else to hand to her, but did neither.

During afternoon break, Madison went to the toilet. As she washed her hands at the sink, Erin emerged from one of the cubicles and they looked at each other in the mirror.

A part of Madison wanted to speak to her. The other part just wanted to run away. She quickly said an internal prayer. 'Dear Jesus, help me to do the right thing. Help me to forgive Erin and invite her to my party.'

"Erin," Madison said as Erin pulled opened the door to leave.

"What?" Erin turned around.

"I just wanted to give you this," Madison said and anxiously removed a pink envelope from her blazer pocket.

"What is it?" Erin asked suspiciously.

"It's an invitation to my party." Madison handed it to her.

"Thanks." Erin snatched it and departed.

Madison felt relieved. She had forgiven Erin in her heart and felt much better for it, even though it had been a very hard thing for her to do.

On the big day Madison got very excited as her friends started arriving at the hall. Their chatter and giggling almost drowned out the music. So when mum called her name, she did not respond until tapped on the shoulder.

"Look who's just arrived," mum said, her eyes sliding towards the entrance.

Madison followed mum's gaze and saw Erin removing her jacket to hang on a peg. Madison rushed over and gave her an enormous hug.

"Hello, Erin. I'm so glad you could make it."

"It was nice of you to invite me." She smiled and handed Madison a card and a present.

"Does this mean we're friends again?" Madison asked.

"We're friends," Erin said. "And I'm sorry for the way I've been acting lately."

"That's all right. It was my fault too."

Madison took her hand and they went to join all the other children. Madison had the best birthday party ever and everybody enjoyed themselves.

"Thank you for making me do the right thing," Madison said to mum at home later.

"Thank you for listening to me, Madison. I'm sure it couldn't have been easy."

"It wasn't."

"It's good to remember that God's way is always the right way and if we live the way he wants us to, everything will turn out for the best in the end."

"And it has," Madison agreed and tucked into another slice of birthday cake.

ANGER

Darren's grandad sat on a wooden bench in the children's play area of the park and watched Darren as he worked his way up the climbing frame. It was a warm and sunny April day.

"Aaaah!"

Darren fell off the frame and landed on his back. Grandad moved as quickly as his arthritic legs would carry him.

"Are you hurt?" grandad asked.

"No," Darren said angrily. "That boy pushed me off."

Grandad looked up to where Darren pointed. A sandy haired boy with freckles grinned down at them.

"Are you sure?"

"Yes. Now I'm going to push *him* off," Darren said, getting up.

"You mustn't do that." Grandad held him.

"Why not?"

"Come on. Let's go over to the swings."

"But I don't want to go on the swings, grandad. I want to go on the climbing frame."

"You can do that later," grandad said firmly.

Darren was still bristling as they approached the swings and waited for someone to get off.

"Here we go," grandad said as a swing became free.

Darren kept an eye on the sandy haired boy as he swung through the air; grandad pushing him occasionally.

"Feeling better?" grandad asked.

Darren didn't answer. He suddenly jumped off the swing, ran towards the roundabout and leapt on as an older boy was about to spin it around.

"Aaaah!"

The sandy haired boy tumbled to the ground. He started crying and his mother rushed over to him.

"What's happened?"

"I was pushed off."

"Who pushed you off?" his mum asked, alarmed.

"Him," the boy pointed at Darren.

"Did you push him off?" she asked him.

"He pushed me off the climbing frame," Darren answered.

"No I didn't. You fell."

"Yes you did," Darren insisted.

"Where's your mother?"

"He's with me," grandad answered, puffing as he approached the roundabout.

"Then I suggest you take better care of him. He pushed my son off the roundabout and he could have had a serious accident."

"I'm very sorry," grandad said. "It won't happen again."

"It better not or I'll go and tell the Park Warden."

"Come on, Darren. Let's go," grandad said and took his hand.

"But I still want to play!"

"I said, let's go," grandad repeated and Darren knew he was in trouble.

"Why did we have to leave?" Darren asked as they headed towards the lake.

"Because you didn't do the right thing back there," grandad said.

"I didn't start it. He did."

"That may be true, but you made matters worse."

"At least he knows what it feels like now."

"And that's important?"

"Yeah. It is."

Grandad sat by the lake and watched a pure white swan as it glided majestically across the water.

"You know, you remind me of me when I was your age."

"How?" Darren asked, beside him.

"I used to have a quick temper too and if anybody messed with me, they soon wished they hadn't. I've had problems controlling my anger for most of my life. In fact, I almost killed a man once."

"What did he do, grandad?"

"Let's just say we had a disagreement over a young lady."

"Grandma?"

"No. It wasn't your grandmother, God rest her soul. It was before we met."

"Did you go to prison for it?"

"I did, but I've never been back."

Darren didn't know what to say. He found this news quite shocking as grandad seemed such a calm and gentle man.

"What happened?"

"Jesus changed me."

"How did he do that?"

"When I asked him to. You see my anger got worse when I came out of prison. I blamed everyone but myself for the things that happened to me. I couldn't hold down a job as I'd end up getting into fights with people. I started drinking heavily and my girlfriend threw me out. Even my parents didn't want me in the house.

I remember walking the streets in the pouring rain one night. It was cold and I had nowhere to go. I looked up to the sky and cried out, 'God, if you're really there, help me. I can't live like this anymore!' Then all of a sudden I felt warmth on my head. A bit like how the sun is shining on us now. It travelled all over my body and I knew that I was in the presence of God. I started telling God how sorry I was for messing up my life and for hurting other people. From that moment on I knew that everything had changed. I felt peace, real peace and joy for the first time in my life."

"Why are you telling me all this, grandad?"

"Because I don't want you to make the same mistakes as me."

"But if I let that boy get away with it, he'd think I was scared of him and I'm not scared of anybody."

"I'm glad to hear that, Darren, but Jesus said, if anyone slaps you on the right cheek, let him slap you on the left cheek too. He also told us to love our enemies and to pray for them."

"I would pray they got run over by a bus."

Grandad chuckled. "That's not what he had in mind. He meant pray good things for them."

"That's too hard."

"It may seem hard, but when we know Jesus, he gives us the power to do what he asks."

"I want that power, grandad."

"Then let's start by praying for that boy. Dear Lord Jesus, we know that you love and care for him as much as you love and care for Darren. Let your love shine on him and his family. Bless his life and we pray that he will turn to you as his Lord and Saviour. I ask this in Jesus' precious name. Amen."

"Amen."

"Now, I think we'd better get back home before your mother arrives to collect you."

"Can I have an ice cream?" Darren asked as they approached an ice cream van.

"As long as I can have one too," grandad answered with a loving smile.

HONESTY

"Who's been drawing on the wall?" dad asked the girls after spotting an inky scrawl above the armchair.

Chloe and Kayla were sitting on the sofa watching cartoons on television and they did not answer. Dad turned the TV off and repeated himself.

"I said who's been drawing on the wall?"

"It wasn't me," said Chloe.

"It wasn't me either," said Kayla.

"So how did it get there? It wasn't there this morning."

"I don't know. But I didn't do it," said Chloe.

"Neither did I," Kayla added.

"One of you is responsible for it and it would be better if whoever did it owned up now. Otherwise you'll both have to be punished."

"Oh, dad," Chloe moaned. "That's not fair."

"It's also not fair that one of you has drawn on the wallpaper and not owned up to it. I may not be able to get it off and I don't know if I've got a spare roll of this paper in the loft to replace it with. Kayla," dad looked his youngest daughter in the eye, "have you got anything to tell me?"

"No, daddy." She stared boldly back at him.

"All right. Both of you go up to your room and stay there until somebody decides to tell me the truth. Go on. Up you go." Dad waved them out, despite their protests. He then went into the kitchen to see if he could find something with which to remove the marks.

When his wife came home she found him cleaning the wall.

"What's happened?" she asked.

"One of the girls has been scribbling on the wall. Nobody's owned up to it, so I've sent them to their room. But I've got most of it out. What do you think?"

"It doesn't look too bad. I'll go up and have a word with them."

"Hello, mum," the girls said as she opened their bedroom door.

"What have you got for us?" Kayla asked mum, who always bought home treats on a Saturday evening after work.

"Nobody gets a treat until somebody tells dad who's scribbled on the living room wall," mum said, then left them to get changed.

Dad was on his laptop in the living room when Kayla crept up to him.

"Sorry, daddy," Kayla whispered into his ear.

"What are you sorry for, Kayla?"

"For drawing on the wall."

"Why did you do that?"

"I don't know."

49

"You've got plenty of paper and colouring books in your room if you want to draw. I don't want this to happen again. Do you understand?"

"Yes, daddy."

"Where's your sister?"

"I'm here." Chloe came in from the passage.

"Good, because I want to talk to both of you."

"What about?" Chloe asked.

"Telling lies."

"I wasn't lying, dad," Chloe insisted.

"Not today, perhaps, but you have on other occasions. Only last week you took my chocolate out of the fridge without asking. We only found out it was you when mum discovered the wrapper under your bed. It's not good to tell lies. God doesn't like it at all, and it can have very serious consequences. I'm sure you've heard the story of 'The boy who cried Wolf.'"

"We know it, dad," said Chloe.

"And what's the moral of the story?"

"That if you keep telling lies, no one will believe you when you're telling the truth," Chloe replied.

"Exactly. So how am I or your mother to know when you're telling the truth if you keep on lying?"

"I didn't want you to be angry with me, daddy," Kayla admitted.

"I can understand why you might not want to tell the truth out of fear of making someone angry or getting into trouble, but it's always better to tell the truth straight away. In fact, you'll find that people will be easier on you and quicker to forgive you if you do. That's because it shows you have taken responsibility for your actions, even though what you did was wrong. If you'd owned up when I first asked you Kayla, I wouldn't have sent you both upstairs. I would have appreciated your honesty. Telling lies is not only bad, it's also very dangerous. People have ended up in prison or been killed because of other people's lies. Pass me the Bible, Chloe."

Chloe got the large children's Bible from the book case and passed it to dad.

"Now can anyone tell me the first lie that was ever told on earth?"

Both girls thought for a moment, but neither came up with an answer.

"Think about the Garden of Eden," dad hinted.

"Oh, I know. It was the snake," Chloe said.

"He got Eve to eat the apple," Kayla elaborated.

"That's right. The serpent told Eve that if she ate from the Tree of the Knowledge of Good and Evil, she wouldn't die. Of course this wasn't true because God made it clear to Adam that they could eat the fruits of any tree in the garden, except that one. He told them they would die if they did. So because she listened to the serpent instead of to

God, Adam and Eve had to leave the garden and that's why everybody has to die."

"That's very sad, daddy," Kayla said.

"It is sad, Kayla, but Jesus is the second Adam and if we believe in him, when we die, we will live again and be with Jesus in heaven. That's the good news."

"I believe in Jesus," Kayla said.

"That's great, Kayla. But belief in Jesus means following his commandments and doing what pleases him. So what does that mean for you? What will you do differently?"

"No more lying."

"And you, Chloe?"

"No more lying, dad."

"Good girls." He gave them both a kiss. "Now go and find out what treat mum has got for you," dad said and the girls flew out of the room.

SACRIFICE

"I haven't heard you practising on the drums lately," dad said to James on opening the living room door.

"I don't need to, dad," James answered as he watched TV.

"I think you do. You begged us to get you a drum kit and all it's doing is taking up space in the dining room."

"I'll practice later," James said.

"Make sure you do, and remember who's paying for the lessons."

"Okay, dad," James replied and dad left him alone. But James didn't practice the drums that evening.

The next day James had a drumming lesson at school with Mr Bush.

"Now let's hear the drum fill," Mr Bush said.

James struggled to follow the music sheet in front of him.

"You should have learnt this by now. Have you been practising?"

"A bit."

"Not enough by the looks of it," Mr Bush gently scolded him. "I was hoping you'd be ready for the school concert, but it looks like I might have to choose somebody else."

But Mr Bush's threats had little effect on him. Every time James thought about practising the drums something else always got in the way, like a programme he wanted to watch, a game he wanted to play or home work to finish.

"Right. TV off," dad said to James a week later.

"But I'm watching something."

"You can record it. I want you on those drums right now or I'm going to sell them."

"All right," James said. He went into the dining room and practiced the drums for half an hour, as he really wanted to play in the school concert.

But later that week, James found out that Mr Bush had chosen Frank to play the drums instead. James was furious. He knew he was a better player than Frank. He sulked all day and was still miserable when mum collected him from the after-school club.

That evening dad joined him in the living room.

"Mum told me you didn't get chosen for the school concert. Do you know the reason why?"

"Because I didn't practice enough."

"And whose fault was that?"

"Mine," James admitted.

"Life is full of distractions, James; perhaps more so now than ever. Apart from Fridays when you go to Scouts, you've got at least two hours in the evenings to do the things that need to be done, and plenty of time at the weekends."

"I know."

"So you need to set yourself a timetable of how you're going to spend your time. I can help you with that. What you need to decide though is what you really value. If being really good at playing the drums is more important than what's on TV, then you are going to have to limit the time spent watching TV."

"I don't even watch that much."

"You watch more than you realise. You'll be a better drummer if you put more time in. It's called making a sacrifice. That's giving up something you value in order to gain something of even greater value. Most successful people have had to make sacrifices in their lives to get to the top of their profession. Can you think of any examples?"

"Footballers."

"That's right. They have to spend hours training every week. That goes for all sports men and women. Some of them have to practice every single day to become champions. Other people make all kinds of sacrifices in order to fulfil their dreams. Even boring old office managers like me have to spend time keeping up with developments by reading documents and attending meetings."

"I will when I'm older."

"But if you don't get into the habit now, you may not be able to later and then you won't achieve the things that God has planned for you. Natural talent isn't always enough. Often it's the people that work the hardest at something who succeed."

"Like Frank Dixon?"

"Yes, like Frank. I'm sure he practiced the drums as much as he could. You don't want to be like the rich young man in the Bible. He asked Jesus what he had to do to have eternal life. Jesus told him to keep the commandments. He said, 'I already do that. What else do I have to do?' Then Jesus told him if he wanted to be perfect, he had to sell everything he owned and give it to the poor, then follow him. This saddened the young man because he was very rich. He valued his earthly possessions more than he valued his reward in heaven.

It isn't always easy to make sacrifices, James, but God rewards us when we do it for the right reasons. There is no easy route to lasting success. We have to fight for it. And do you know who made the biggest sacrifice of all?"

"No."

"It was Jesus. He came to earth as a man and died on the cross so that all those who believed in him would have ever lasting life. In this way he defeated death. Don't you think it was a price worth paying?"

"I do."

"Then let's pray about it. Dear Lord Jesus, thank you for James's gift for playing the drums. I pray that you will help him understand the need to make sacrifices in life in order to achieve the desires of his heart, which you have placed within him. I also pray that he becomes a skilful drummer through regular practice and plays for your glory. Amen."

"Amen," James said. "I'm going to start practising right now."

"Good boy," dad said, beaming.

James got into the habit of practising the drums regularly and a few months later he entered the school talent contest. Mr Bush set up the drum kit on stage and when James's name was called, gave him lots of encouragement.

James amazed the audience with his drumming that evening and he received rapturous applause. Mum and dad were very proud of him and James was happy that the sacrifices he'd made had been worth it.

FAITH

"We're going to be late," Esther said, anxiously wringing her hands.

"Don't worry. Cherry will be here soon," mum assured her.

"What time is it now?"

"Five to ten," mum said, after looking at her watch.

"What time was Cherry supposed to be here?" Esther asked.

"Quarter to. If she isn't here in five minutes, I'll give her a call."

"Okay."

"Do you want to go over any of your pieces again while we're waiting?"

"No, mum. I just want to go." Esther was standing in the hallway.

A few minutes later, mum called Cherry's mobile phone, but it went to voicemail, so she left her a message.

"Why don't we get a cab, mum?"

"It's too late for that. I'm sure Cherry's on her way, otherwise she would have rung us if she couldn't make it."

"Maybe something's happened to her and she can't contact us."

"She's probably stuck in traffic."

"That means I'm definitely going to miss my exam."

"Not necessarily. Have a bit of faith."

"How can I when I'm stressed?"

"When we're stressed is exactly when we need to have faith in God and to trust him."

"Oh, this is driving me crazy!" Esther cried. "What time is it now?"

"Nearly ten past."

"Mum, I have to be there at ten thirty!"

"I know."

"Why don't you ring the music school and tell them we're going to be late?"

"I could do that, I suppose," mum said and took the letter out of her bag to get their telephone number. She was waiting for the phone to be answered, when the doorbell rang.

Esther opened the front door to Cherry and they hurried out.

"I'm really sorry I didn't phone," Cherry said after Esther's mum had finished her call. "I took my phone off charge this morning and must have left it on the bed. I only found out I didn't have it when I hit temporary traffic lights. By then it was too late to turn back."

"That's all right. You did give Esther a bit of a fright, though," mum said, with a smile.

"Sorry, Esther."

"That's okay."

By God's grace they had light traffic on their journey and were only held up briefly by one red light. They arrived at ten thirty on the dot and the child whose name was listed before Esther's had just been called.

They waited in a large hall that contained three pianos, one of which was being beautifully played by a young girl.

"Why don't you have a little practice?" mum encouraged Esther.

"I'll probably muck it up," Esther answered.

"No you won't," mum said crossly. "I don't want you talking like that."

Esther just had time to practice her scales before being called.

"Good luck, Esther," Cherry said.

"Have faith and remember that God is with you," mum said.

"I'll try," Esther said and followed the woman out of the room.

"How did it go?" mum asked Esther on her return.

"I think it went all right," Esther said smiling.

"You see. Now let's get you back to school," mum said, as they left.

Cherry treated Esther to a milkshake on the way.

"Now tell me what good all that worrying did you?" mum asked, as they drove off again.

"I can't," Esther admitted after sucking up the sweet, thick liquid through a straw.

"That's because worrying is a waste of energy. We need to give all our concerns to God, for when we do that we're no longer trying to do things in our own strength, but in his. When we're weak, he's strong."

"That's right," said Cherry. "I remember when I worried myself sick about Robert when he started getting into all kinds of trouble as a teenager.

I tried everything I could think of to get him straightened out, but nothing seemed to work. I met your mum in a keep fit class one day and she invited me to her church. I wasn't a believer at the time, but the moment I walked in, I felt at peace. The pastor talked about having faith and trusting in God for everything, and I knew that I needed to do that with Robert. I prayed for him and believed God would change him. I declared it every day until little by little, I saw changes in his behaviour. He stopped hanging around with certain people and seemed calmer, less confrontational. That, in part, was due to the fact that God was changing *me*. I stopped trying to control him.

Maybe that's why he accepted my invitation to come to church with me when I asked him. He's now a Christian and serves in the youth ministry."

"Praise God," mum said.

"But we all have different levels of faith, and God said if we only have faith as big as a mustard seed, which is really tiny, we can do anything. That's worth remembering," Cherry said.

"I'll try and remember that next time," Esther said.

"But sometimes we need big faith, don't we?" mum said.

"Yes. Especially when we're called to step out in faith," Cherry added.

"What does that mean?" Esther asked.

"It's when God asks us to do something and we have no idea how it's going to be done," said Cherry. "Like when Jesus walked on water and asked Peter to get out of the boat and come to him. He started off all right, but when he looked at his surroundings, a lack of belief and fear set in and he started to sink. Stepping out in faith can feel uncomfortable at first, because we're doing something new. But if we keep our eyes firmly fixed on Jesus, even though it won't always be easy, we'll succeed in the end," Cherry said and pulled up near Esther's school.

"Thanks, Cherry," Esther said, getting out of the car. She said goodbye to mum when the school gate opened, and felt encouraged to know that with faith in God, anything was possible.

GIVING

"I thought I told you to put all your old toys in a bag for me," mum said, on entering Dominic's room.

"I sorted the clothes out," Dominic said.

"Yes, I can see that, but there's only one book in this other bag and look, some of the pages are torn, so we'll have to chuck it away."

"I haven't got anything else to put in there."

"I'm sure you have. Let's see," mum said and opened the cupboard door. It contained an assortment of toys, crayons, puzzles, books, and sports equipment.

"We're going to have to take everything out," mum said.

"Oh, mum! Why can't we leave it as it is?"

"Because it's a mess and what we don't throw away, we can give to charity."

"But I want to keep *everything*."

"You can keep a few things, but that's it."

"But they're *mine!*"

"That's true, but you don't play with any of these things any more. You've outgrown them. Don't you think it's better that other people get to make use of them?"

"Other people can go to the shops and buy things for themselves."

"But some people don't have much money to spend on their children, or have family that can either."

"That's not my fault."

"Dominic, it's good to give things to other people. That's what God wants us to do. The Bible says, 'It's more blessed to give than to receive.' "

"Well, I think it's better to get than to give. That's why I like Christmas and birthdays, when I get lots of presents. I'm going to keep that," Dominic said, grabbing a Spider Man figure.

"Jesus also said, 'Give to others and God will give to you.' "

"What will he give to me?"

"It's different for everyone. For some people it will be the sheer pleasure of giving and serving God. For others it will be favour in another area of their life or answered prayers. The possibilities are endless. It's worth testing out to see what happens."

"Okay, mum. I will."

"But remember, 'God loves a cheerful giver.' That means you shouldn't give begrudgingly."

"I get it," Dominic said.

That weekend, Dominic bought a big bag of sweets and brought them to school. He gave them to Mr Jackson to hand out to the class.

"You didn't tell me it was your birthday," Jayden said, as they ate lunch in the dining hall.

"It isn't," Dominic replied.

"Then why did you bring in the sweets?"

"I just felt like it."

"Okay." Jayden looked at him suspiciously.

"But seeing as how I did, can I have your apple crumble and custard?"

"No."

"Why not?"

"Because I want it and you've got your own."

"The Bible says, 'It's better to give than to receive.' "

"Yeah, well I'll be giving you a mouthful of knuckles if you're not careful," Jayden said and everyone on the table laughed.

Dominic was in a bad mood for the rest of the day. So much for giving. He wouldn't be doing that again in a hurry.

"What's wrong?" mum asked when she picked him up from the After School Club. Dominic told her what had happened during the short car journey home.

"Oh, Dominic," mum said as she parked up on the drive. "You're not supposed to give just so that you can get what you want from someone. That's not what I was saying."

They entered the house, where Dominic threw off his shoes and blazer and followed his mum into the kitchen.

"When you give, it has to be out of the goodness of your heart; not because you expect something in return," mum said as she began preparing the evening meal.

"Maybe I haven't got a good heart," Dominic muttered.

"Of course you have." Mum turned to face him. "Being a Christian is about doing right, not feeling right. The more we read the Bible, the more we get to understand God's nature and how he rewards us when we do his work. If we get thanks from people, that's fine, but if we don't get thanks, well that's fine too. And there's many ways of giving, you know."

"What ways?"

"Being helpful around the house for a start."

"What do you want me to do, mum?"

"Nothing at the moment. But just think about how you can give to others when you're at home or school or anywhere. Be a good friend and say things that are kind and encouraging. It's a question of seeing a need and meeting it. As a ten year old, God isn't expecting you to give what you haven't got, but to give what you do have. We can all make a difference in someone else's life. We just have to choose to. Do you think you can do that?"

"I suppose so."

At that moment the front door banged shut as Amy, Dominic's sixteen year-old sister came home.

"Hi, mum," she said as she whizzed past the kitchen and sprang up the stairs to her room.

"Hi, love," mum replied, then asked Dominic if he had any home work to do.

"Just a bit," he told her.

"Well I think you'd better go up and do it," mum said.

"Can't I do it later?"

"It's best to get it out of the way and then you can relax later."

"Okay, mum," Dominic said and went out.

Half an hour later, Amy came down and entered the kitchen.

"Mum, is something wrong with Dom?"

"Not that I know of. Why, what's the matter?"

"He asked me if he could do anything for me. I told him to go away and leave me alone. When I asked him what he wanted, he said he didn't want anything. I said there has to be a catch and he said there wasn't one. So I asked him to bring me up a drink and he did. It was really weird."

"Well, you'd better get used to it," mum said, laughing. "Your brother's learning about giving and he's starting with you."

WORD POWER

"How was school today?" mum asked
Hannah as they went through the gate at home time.

"It was quite fun, actually. Miss Castle got so
upset with the class that she had a bit of a fit."

"That's not very good, is it?"

"It was funny though."

"I'm sure it wasn't very funny for Miss
Castle."

"She's such a rubbish teacher."

"Why are you saying that?"

"Because she doesn't know how to teach and
she doesn't know how to control the boys properly."

"That's not a very nice thing to say, Hannah."

"But it's true."

"You're always saying nasty things about Miss Castle and it's not respectful. I don't get the impression she's such a bad teacher."

"That's because you don't have to spend all day with her."

"Even so, Hannah, I want you to stop speaking about her like that. I'm sure that's why she tells me you've got an attitude problem."

"She just likes picking on me."

"I'm sure there's a very good reason."

"It's not my fault she's a bad teacher."

"She's a young teacher and still finding her feet. Anyway, you're responsible for how you behave. You don't have to follow the crowd. If she asks you to do something, then you need to listen to her and do it."

"I think she'll get the sack soon." Hannah giggled.

"Hannah, you really do need to think about what you're saying. Words have power," mum said as they stood at the curb waiting to cross the road. "What you say affects other people," she continued, once they were safely over.

"Sticks and stones…" Hannah began.

"'May break my bones, but words will never hurt me,'" mum finished. "Yes, we used to say that when I was at school. But it's not true. Words do hurt us. Words go deeper than actual wounds."

"That's probably why Cora and Alice had a fight today; because Cora called Alice a big fat pig."

"My point exactly. You kids can be very cruel to each other. You need to think about whether what you say is going to help or hinder a person; whether it's something good to hear or bad."

"We had an assembly about cyber bullying this morning."

"I remember seeing the email. It's becoming a growing problem at school. At least in the past bullying stopped in the playground, but with modern technology it's never ending."

"When I get a nasty text, I just delete it."

"But not everybody's as strong as you, Hannah. For somebody who already lacks confidence it can be devastating and tip them over the edge. I'm sure you're aware that occasionally it has led to a child taking their own life."

"I know."

"And I hope you're not saying or texting unpleasant things to other people."

"I'm not mum, so don't worry."

"Good, because our words have the power to bring about good or evil; life or death. So we have to be careful about what we say to ourselves and about ourselves, let alone what we say to and about others. Start thinking about some good things we could say to people."

"We could pay them a compliment."

"That's a good idea. People always remember compliments, as long as you mean them. What else?"

"Be kind to my friends."

"I'm sure you already are, but you need to be kind to the people who aren't your friends as well."

"I can't think of anything else."

"Well, when your friends are saying bad things about someone, instead of joining in, you could say something nice about them or change the subject."

"That could be tricky."

"I know, but it's worth a try. It's what God would want you to do. The Bible tells us we will have to answer for every useless word we have ever spoken, so it's good to start putting that right as soon as possible. I know we all say rude or hurtful things to others at times, especially when we're upset or angry, but we can ask God to forgive us when we do."

They had reached their front door. Mum put her key in the lock and they entered.

"I want you to think about one good thing you can say about Miss Castle," mum said as Hannah followed her into the kitchen.

"I can't think of anything."

"She's got nice green eyes."

"I haven't noticed."

"Well, have a good look at her tomorrow and try to find one nice thing to say about her. If you really look I'm sure you'll find something."

"Okay."

"And remember that we all have faults Hannah; you included. That's why the Bible says we're to take the log out of our own eyes before we can see clearly to take the speck out of our brother's eyes. I want to pray with you about it right now," mum said and put her hands on Hannah's shoulders. "Dear Lord Jesus, I give you thanks for Hannah's life, her health, and strong character. I pray Lord that you will give her a humble, uncritical heart and that her words will build others up, and not knock them down. I ask this in Jesus' name. Amen."

"Amen."

"Now go and get changed and think about what I've been saying."

"Thanks for praying for me, mum."

"And pray for Miss Castle. Pray that she becomes a really good teacher."

"It'll take a lot of praying."

"Then you'd best get started," mum replied.

The following day at home time, Hannah was in a buoyant mood as she emerged from her classroom.

"You were right about Miss Castle's eyes. They *are* quite nice," Hannah said to mum. "And she actually made us laugh today."

"How did she do that?"

"She told us a funny story about her family."

Mum smiled and silently praised God.

PRIDE

Max looked forward to seeing his uncle Tony, who hadn't been around in ages. He couldn't remember ever going to his uncle's place and didn't think his mum had been there either as she used the 'sat nav' to find it.

His uncle was surprised to see them and hesitated before letting them in.

"The place is in a bit of a mess at the moment, I'm afraid," he said.

Max had to move all sorts of papers and clothes before he could sit on the sofa and watch TV. His mum and uncle went into the kitchen to talk and there were raised voices on both sides. They emerged half an hour later.

"I'll sort it out," said uncle Tony.

"When?" asked mum.

"When I'm ready to."

"And when will that be? When the bailiffs come knocking?"

"I said I'd sort it."

"Okay." Mum sighed with frustration. "Come on, Max, we'd better get going."

"What's the matter, mum?" Max asked as they descended the concrete steps that led out of the building.

"Your uncle Tony has got some serious problems that he's not facing up to."

"What sort of problems?"

"Money problems," mum said as they approached her car.

"Why?"

"Because he's lost his job and hasn't been able to find another one."

"Is that why we haven't seen him lately?"

"Probably. He didn't want me to know."

"Why not?"

"Pride, I suppose."

"What's pride?"

"It can mean thinking you're better than other people or in your uncle's case not asking for help when you need it."

"Does he need help to tidy up the flat?"

"No, he can do that for himself," mum said as she joined the motorway.

"What help does he need then?" Max wondered.

"He needs money to pay his rent; otherwise he could get thrown out of there."

"Who'll throw him out?"

"His landlord. That's the person he has to pay the rent to."

"Can you give him the money, mum?"

"I wish I could, but he owes quite a lot."

"Can anyone else help?"

"There is help out there, but he keeps thinking he'll find a job soon, so he's not doing anything. He's a very stubborn person; always has been. Even when he was little. I remember dad driving us to Southend when Tony was seven and I was ten. We were sitting in the back and when I put my hand down on the seat, it felt damp. Your uncle Tony had wet himself and he didn't say anything. He just sat there, hoping no one would notice." Max laughed. "I wasn't very amused at the time, I can tell you and neither were mum and dad. Pride isn't a good thing and God hates it."

"Why?"

"Because no one is better than anybody else. We all have our strengths and weaknesses and God wants us to be humble, which is the opposite of pride. Being humble is accepting that we don't know everything and when we get things wrong to admit it and ask for help when we need it."

"We've got a boy in our class who's a know - it - all. He's always showing off about something and never lets you speak. He always tries to make you look stupid. I don't really like him and I don't think many people do, as he hasn't got any close friends."

"That's a shame. He probably doesn't realise that his attitude is driving people away. Nobody wants to be made to feel less important than anyone else and everybody deserves to be listened to. We learn a lot from each other when we do that.

The story of the prodigal son in the Bible is a good example of someone who was full of pride. He thought he knew best. He wanted his inheritance from his father, and went off to a foreign country. He had a good time and friends, until all his money ran out. He ended up accepting a job looking after pigs. No one cared for him and he was hungry. He started thinking about his father's servants and how they always had enough food to eat. He decided to swallow his pride and go back to his father's house as a servant. It was a wise decision as his father was waiting to welcome him with open arms and they had a feast in honour of his return."

"I like that story."

"It's a powerful one and has another meaning, which is that God welcomes us back and rejoices when we stray from him. I think this is a good time to pray for uncle Tony. Do you want to do it?"

"Okay. I'll pray," Max said. He put his hands together and closed his eyes. "Dear Jesus, I pray that uncle Tony will be humble and ask for the help he needs so that he can keep his home. Amen."

"Amen."

A couple of days later, Max's mum got a phone call from uncle Tony.

"I just wanted you to know that I've signed on at the job centre and I've spoken to the landlord."

"That's great. What did the landlord say?"

"Well, he wasn't very happy that I hadn't been returning his calls or responding to his letters.

But he said I was a good tenant and he didn't really want me to leave."

"Does that mean he's not going to evict you?"

"That's right, as long as he receives the rent from now on."

"That's wonderful news."

"Thanks for coming to see me when you did, sis."

"I'm glad I did. Just make sure you get that flat cleaned up."

"I've already started," he laughed.

Once off the phone, mum told Max the good news.

"Hooray!" Max clapped his hands together. "Thank you God, for answering our prayers. Now we need to pray that uncle Tony finds a new job."

"That's a great idea. Let's do that," mum agreed.

GOD IS WATCHING

"Anita?" Mum knocked on Anita's bedroom door and entered. She found her daughter lying in bed fully clothed. "Anita, I want to talk to you."

"I want to watch TV."

"You know you can't watch TV this evening."

"Why not?"

"Because you're being punished. Now up you get." Anita reluctantly peeled back the duvet and sat up. "I sent you upstairs to do some reading, not to go to bed."

"I don't feel like reading."

"That may be the case, but it's something you have to do. Just like you knew you had to revise for the spelling test and didn't."

"Oh, mum!"

"I'm sorry Anita, but I'm really disappointed in your behaviour. Cheating is a very serious matter."

"It was only a spelling test, mum."

"And the consequences have been failing to get a mark and getting a detention. You wouldn't be in all this trouble if you'd put the work in."

"I know."

"But are you sorry, Anita?"

"I said I was sorry."

"Are you sorry that you did it in the first place or just sorry you got caught?"

"I won't do it again."

"I hope not. I was really shocked when Miss Graham told me what you'd done. She'll be watching you like a hawk from now on too. You used to show me the words you had to learn and we'd go through them together. You're quite good at spelling. There was no need to cheat."

"I only did it because I left the paper in my book bag and didn't have time to revise."

"But you had time to copy the words onto a bit of paper and put it in your sock though, didn't you? Why on earth did you think you'd get away with it?"

"I didn't think anybody would notice."

"People always think that no one will notice or find out about their wrong doing when they do it in secret, but God has a way of ensuring that whatever is covered up is revealed. We hear about these things on the news all the time. A person gets caught for crimes committed many years ago. They thought they'd got away with it and were safe, but they were wrong."

"Ronan was spying on me."

"Not necessarily. He saw what he was supposed to see, which was a blessing in disguise. Imagine for a minute that no one saw what you were doing in class. You'd be feeling very pleased with yourself and think you were clever to have got away with it. You'd want to cheat again and again and the more you got away with it, the more confident you'd feel and take greater risks until eventually you'd be caught. It never pays to cheat.

There was a married couple in the Bible who tried to cheat God and things didn't work out too well for them." Mum picked up the children's Bible from Anita's dressing table and found the story of Ananias and Sapphira. "Here it is. This couple sold their property and were supposed to give all the money they got for it to the church, because all Christians shared everything they had in those days. But this couple decided to keep some of the money back for themselves. But the husband was found out by Peter, one of Jesus' disciples."

"How?"

"Through discernment. That's sensing something without being told by anybody and is a gift of the Holy Spirit. Now because Ananias was found guilty of lying to God, he dropped down dead. Then they brought his wife in and questioned her about the money they'd received for the property. She lied just like her husband, and dropped down dead too! Now I'm not saying these things to frighten you, Anita, but to make you understand that God sees everything we do and we cannot hide from him. When you cheated on your spelling test you were cheating yourself out of a good education. You see getting top marks is one thing, but if you don't really know what you should, at some point this will be tested. Then everyone will find out the truth about you. Imagine how you'd feel then?"

"I'd feel pretty bad, I suppose."

"That's right. You don't want people to think of you as a cheat, do you?"

"No."

"That's why it's always better to do your homework and work as hard as you can. Never be afraid to fail because we can learn from our mistakes."

"But you've always wanted me to do well in *everything*."

"I must admit that your dad and I have probably focused too much on results and I'll have a talk with him about it later. But we love you for who you are, not for how well you do. Just remember that God is watching us all the time and if he's watching you, then he's certainly watching me. I have to be aware of my own behaviour and how I treat people. When I get it wrong, God lets me know by reminding me of what I did or didn't do and I won't feel right about it inside. That's because I know I haven't pleased God, and as a Christian I always want to do that, whether anybody's watching me or not. I ask God to forgive me, and if I've been unkind to someone, if it's at all possible, I go back to that person and apologize to them."

"I promise never to cheat again, mum," Anita said and this time she meant it.

"I'm glad to hear it. Come on, let's go down and watch some TV," mum said.

"No thanks. I think I'll do some reading," Anita said, reaching for her school library book.

"Then I'll leave you to get on with it," mum said and quietly closed the bedroom door behind her.

TEMPTATION

"There's Michael Jacobs. He's the one that punched me in the mouth at home time yesterday," Kieran said, tugging onto his dad's arm as they moved towards the restaurant exit.

Michael and his dad had just been seated and were examining the menu when two angry faces appeared at their table.

"Look what your boy did to my son's face!" Kieran's dad thrust his son forward and pointed to his swollen lip.

"Sorry?" Michael's dad frowned as other customers conversations died down to focus on their table.

"You heard me. Your son is a bully and if he lays another finger on my son he'll have me to answer to. Do you hear me?" He glared at Michael.

"Hold on a minute. Can we just hold it right there?" Michael's dad kept his voice firm and even. "Michael, did you do this to him?"

"Yes." Michael answered defiantly.

"Why?"

"Because... because I just did."

"You see. He's no better than an animal," Kieran's dad continued. "He needs to be taught a lesson."

"And I will do just that, right after he apologises. Michael?"

"I've got nothing to say," Michael replied his eyes focused on the menu.

"Michael," dad slammed his palm down on the table, "I'm beginning to lose my patience with you. Say sorry now and be quick about it."

This seemed to rouse the boy and he apologised but without sincerity.

"I'm going to take this up with the school first thing on Monday morning, and I'm going to make sure your son gets kicked out of there! Come on," Kieran's dad said. When they left, everyone started talking again.

Dad considered abandoning their meal as a punishment, but then decided that this was the perfect place to get his son's full attention. He let out a long and painful sigh.

"Now tell me what that was all about?"

"There's nothing to tell."

"I want to know why you hit that boy."

"We don't like Kieran."

"Who's *we*?"

At that moment, the waitress came over, took their order and removed the menus, leaving nothing for Michael to hide behind.

"Well?" dad asked.

"All of us."

"Who's all of us?"

"Liam and the others."

"Who's this Liam?"

"He's the new boy. He's a good mate."

"And how did you get on with Kieran before Liam came to the school?"

"All right, I suppose."

"So what's changed?"

"He got Liam into trouble."

"How?"

"He told the teacher what he'd been doing."

"And what had he been doing?"

"Nothing much. Just having a laugh, that's all."

"And what do you call having a laugh?"

"He was throwing stones at the houses that back onto the playground."

"I hope you weren't doing that."

"I was only watching."

"Are you sure?"

"Yes, dad."

"Did Liam tell you to hit the boy?"

"He dared me."

"And what do you think would have happened if you hadn't done it?"

"Liam and the others wouldn't want to be my friend anymore."

"Would that have been such a bad thing?"

"Of course. Liam's the coolest kid in my class."

"But he's also a bad influence," dad said sadly. "Look at the mess you're in now."

"I didn't know we'd see Kieran and his dad in here."

"No, you didn't. But that's the problem when you go around hurting people. You never know when or where you'll see them or what they'll do to get even. Why did Liam leave his last school?"

"His mum had to leave the area. That's all he told me."

"I know you like Liam, but he dared you to do something that was wrong and you gave in to that temptation because you wanted his friendship, whatever the cost. You're in year six now and come September you'll be in big school. If you do the wrong thing because people like Liam, tell you to, you won't have much of a future. That's how people end up going to prison."

"Oh, dad," Michael scoffed. "I'm not a criminal."

"I didn't say you were. I just want you to understand that the trouble with sin is that it starts off with little things. At first you believe you're in control. But before long the sin overtakes you and eventually leads to your destruction. That's how young people get into addictions like smoking, drinking, drug taking or other criminal activities.

It's always easy to get into something, but much harder to get out of it. We all face temptations every single day, but if we know God, we know we have the power to resist it. You do this by focusing on what the Bible says, just like Jesus did when the devil tempted him in the wilderness.

It also concerns me that you thought Liam throwing stones into someone's garden was a laugh. You should have thought about whether someone could have been in their garden and seriously hurt or had one of their windows broken. You've always got to think about the possible consequences of your actions."

"I'm sorry, dad," Michael said, feeling genuinely ashamed of himself.

"As for Liam, the best thing you can do is to pray for him."

"What should I pray for?"

"Pray that Jesus will come into his life and bless him and his family. And I'll pray that you'll do what God wants you to and not give in to temptation. Remember the words of the Lord's Prayer: 'Lead us not into temptation, but deliver us from evil.' I want you to say that prayer every morning before you go to school."

"Will I really have to leave the school, dad?"

"With God's grace, you won't. But you will have to be punished, and on Monday I want you to really say sorry to Kieran and to be kind to him from now on."

"Okay, dad. I will."

"Oh look, here come our pizza's," dad said, and Michael rubbed his hands together with relish.

.

WISDOM

The man watched Elise approaching his car. Ben, her fifteen year-old brother, had passed by moments earlier, chatting with two friends. The man pushed back his hoodie and lowered the window.

"Hi, Elise," he said, much to her surprise.

"Do I know you?" Elise stopped to ask.

"Yeah. I'm a friend of your mum's."

"Hi." She gave him a little wave.

"Your mum called me up a few minutes ago and asked me to collect you from school."

"Oh, that's okay. My brother picked me up."

"Your mother's not very well."

105

"What do you mean?" Elise's heart began pounding.

"She's had an accident."

"Oh no! Is she okay?"

"She's been taken to hospital. That's why she asked me to pick you up. Now get in quickly and I'll take you to see her right away."

"But what about my brother? I need to tell him."

"Hop in and I'll turn around and pick him up on the way. The door's open."

She was about to reach for the passenger door when she heard her name being called and saw Ben and his friends racing back towards her.

The man started the engine, pressed hard on the accelerator and shot off down the road and spun around the corner, tyres screeching.

"Are you all right?" Ben asked her, breathing heavily.

"I don't know," Elise said as she trembled uncontrollably from the shock.

106

"Praise God for Troy," mum said to Elise as they sat on a sandy beach.

"Why, what did he do?" Elise asked as she scooped sand into a plastic bucket.

"He was your guardian angel that day. He turned around and saw that you weren't behind them. That's when they all turned around and spotted you down the road by that man's car."

"What will happen to him now?"

"His case will go to court and he'll go to prison, so that he can't try to hurt anybody else."

"I feel sorry for him in a way," Elise said and tipped the bucket deep into the sand.

"I pray he gets the help that he needs," mum said with some difficulty. "As for your brother, I've told him that you need to walk in front of him in future, so that he can see you at all times."

"It's not Ben's fault, mum."

"I know it isn't. But he was responsible for your safety."

"It sounds silly now, but I was just worried about you being hurt."

"I know you were darling. You're a very caring person. But if I did ever have an accident, your dad or aunt would be contacted first, and they'd contact your school and Ben's."

"I wish I'd thought about that at the time," Elise said.

"Don't worry about it. Anyone can get caught out. It doesn't matter whether you're young or old. There'll always be evil people out there, both men and women, who want to trick others for their own ends. They often use the element of surprise to catch us off guard. That's why we need to ask God for wisdom. The Bible says wisdom was created before God made the world. Did you know that?"

"No." Elise paused. "What *is* wisdom?"

"It's the opposite of being foolish."

"So it's being sensible?"

"Partly. It's also being careful and cautious. It's thinking in a way that makes use of our experience, knowledge and understanding, so that we make the right decisions. Like you remembering not to fill your glass to the top, because you know from experience that you'll end up spilling your drink everywhere. For me it might mean not speeding or driving through a red light because I know it's wrong and could cause a serious accident. We need to use wisdom every single day of our lives, in our speech as well as our actions."

"Sometimes I know what's right, but I don't do it," Elise confessed.

"We're all guilty of doing that, because we're all sinners who want to please ourselves instead of God. That's why Jesus says in the Bible: 'The spirit is willing but the flesh is weak.' There's a constant battle going on. But God is good and can speak to us through our five senses. Can you name them?"

"Um, let me see. There's sight, hearing, touch, taste and smell."

"Well done. There's also something called the sixth sense or intuition. It's where someone knows or understands something in a way which cannot be explained naturally. The Bible calls it discernment. God can suddenly reveal something to us through the Holy Spirit. It might be just a feeling that something isn't quite right about a person or a place. If there's even the slightest doubt, we need to step back and if necessary walk away."

"At least everyone at school knows how to keep themselves safe now."

"Yes. That newsletter was really useful. Are you having a good time?" Elise nodded. "Shane, Ben!" mum called to them as they played with a Frisbee.

Father and son weaved their way past other sun seekers to join them.

"I want to pray for us," mum said after a few minutes. "Dear heavenly Father, thank you for my husband and two beautiful children. I thank you that we're all together enjoying the sunshine on this glorious day. I pray that you will give each one of us your godly wisdom, which you said is better than silver or gold, better than jewels and better than an inheritance. I also pray that Elise continues to grow closer to you and flourishes into the intelligent, talented person that you have called her to be. I bind all the works of the enemy over this family in the mighty name of Jesus Christ, Amen."

"Amen," they all chimed.

At that moment a donkey to ride was being paraded across the sand.

"Oh can I have a ride on the donkey?" Elise asked, excitedly.

"Yes, of course you can," mum said, and stood up to accompany her daughter.

HEARING FROM GOD

"Get your jacket on, we're going to the shops," gran told Elliott, who was immersed in a football match on his games console.

"I've got to finish this match, gran," Elliott answered, his thumbs tapping frantically away on the pads.

"It'll have to wait. We've got to go now." Gran already had her coat and shoes on.

"But we went shopping yesterday."

"I know, but there's something I want to buy."

"All right." Elliott let out an enormous sigh.

Ten minutes later they arrived at the local supermarket. Gran bought some vegetables and let Elliott choose a cake from the bakery. At the checkout, only one person was in front of them and his items had been scanned and bagged. The cashier waited patiently for the elderly man to pay for his goods. He mumbled as he searched his coat pockets and trousers for his wallet.

"I know I've got my wallet here, somewhere," he said to the cashier.

"Take your time." The young female cashier gave him a reassuring smile.

"I hope I haven't dropped it anywhere."

"Do you want me to call someone to have a look for it in the shop?" the cashier asked.

"No, no. I'll just leave the stuff here. I'll go home and come back with the money."

"Are you sure?"

"Yes. That's what I'll do."

"How much is it?" gran suddenly asked the cashier.

"Eleven pounds and twenty pence."

"I'll pay for it," gran said and gave the cashier a twenty pound note.

"You don't have to do that," the man said. "I'll come back."

But gran told the cashier to go ahead with the payment.

"You're a good woman," the man smiled, showing small yellowy teeth.

"It's no problem."

"God bless you," he said, took his shopping and hobbled away.

"Why did you pay for that man's shopping, gran?" Elliott asked as they walked home.

"Because God told me to."

"God doesn't talk to people."

"He talks to us all the time."

"How do you know it's God?"

"I can recognise his voice; just like I know your dad's voice when he phones me."

"What does God sound like?"

"He often sounds just like me." Elliot looked confused. "We talk to ourselves in our heads all the time, don't we? And thoughts pop into our heads, both good and bad that we can't control. Well, those good thoughts are from God. They could be a suggestion, an idea, an instruction or the answer to a problem."

"And what did God tell you about that man?"

"He didn't tell me anything about him. He just told me to go to that shop straight away. I knew I was going to help somebody, but I didn't know who."

"That's pretty cool."

"Sometimes he speaks to us as if there's someone nearby. That's how he spoke to Samuel in the Bible, when he was a boy. When God called his name, he thought Eli was calling him from the next room. God speaks to us in many different ways."

"What other ways, gran?"

"He sometimes talks to us through other people; even strangers."

"Has that ever happened to you, gran?"

"Once or twice. I remember having an important decision to make and two separate people confirmed what I should do, without them even knowing my plans."

"That's amazing."

"God can also talk to us through pictures that we see in our minds or in dreams or visions."

"What are visions?"

"It's being awake, but seeing something in front of you that other people can't see."

"Like seeing a ghost?"

"More like a film in front of your eyes."

"That's fantastic."

"I'm sure it is."

"Have you had a vision, gran?"

"No, I haven't."

"How else does God talk to us?"

"Through our senses and feelings. Sometimes we feel uncomfortable around someone, even when there's no obvious reason. We always need to listen to these feelings to keep ourselves safe. Then of course there's through reading the Bible. Have you been reading that Bible I gave you?"

"Not much."

"Bring it with you the next time you come round. You see the more we read God's words, the more we learn about God and his nature."

"How else does God speak?"

"Through answered prayers and not just the big prayers, but the little, everyday ones."

Elliott was quiet when they arrived back at gran's house and he slumped onto the sofa.

"Did you enjoy our little talk, Elliott?"

"It was all right, gran, but God doesn't speak to me."

"Of course he does. You just haven't been tuning in to his wavelength, that's all. We have so much information buzzing around in our heads these days, that people have forgotten how to listen to God and he really wants to talk to us."

"What can I do to hear him, gran?"

"You can ask God a question."

"What sort of question?"

"Something you want to know the answer to. But don't tell me, tell God. Sit up properly and close your eyes." Elliott did as he was told. "Be very quiet and empty your mind. Just focus on God and who he is: the Creator of the universe. He also created you. Ask him a question, and then wait for an answer. It might be a word or a picture. Don't dismiss whatever comes to mind and when you're ready, open your eyes and tell me what happened."

"I asked God if he could speak to me the way he speaks to you, gran." Elliott said a few minutes later.

"And what did he answer?"

"He showed me a picture of a mobile phone. What d'you think it means, gran?"

"Well, what's the purpose of a mobile phone?"

"To talk to people."

"That's right. It's for taking and making calls and I believe God is saying you already have what you need to communicate with him. Don't you agree?"

"I do now. God spoke to me!"

"And he always will," gran said and gave Elliott a massive hug.

PRAYER

"Oh, I really hope it doesn't rain today," Mia said, looking up at the grey, cloudy sky, as dad walked her to school.

"Maybe you should pray about it," dad suggested.

"That won't work."

"Why not? Doesn't God answer prayers?"

"Sometimes, but he can't change the weather!"

"God can do whatever we ask, as long as it's his will. Do you remember when we were on the

120

train the other day and that drunken man got on and sat opposite us?"

"He really scared me."

The man was much bigger than Mia's dad. He wore dirty jeans and a T-shirt and his breath smelt of beer. He ranted one minute and was singing the next.

"Can we move?" Mia had whispered in her dad's ear.

Dad responded by a shake of the head, but put a comforting arm around her.

The man started singing again at the top of his lungs, laughed and then settled back in his seat. His eye lids fluttered several times before they remained closed and he fell asleep.

When they'd got off the train, dad told her how he'd prayed for the man to be quiet.

"God heard my prayer and he answered it," dad said as they now waited to cross a busy junction.

"I was really glad about that," Mia said. "But the weather affects lots of people. What if I pray for it to be dry and somebody else prays for it to rain?"

"That's a good question. But it can be dry in one area and be raining in another, even within the same city."

"Really?"

"It happens all the time. And remember, God answers little prayers and big prayers because he delights in giving good things to his children. There's a wonderful story in the Bible that illustrates the power of prayer. It's when Peter was put in prison for spreading the good news about Jesus. The night before he was due to be put on trial, an angel appeared in his prison cell and woke him up; told him to get dressed and follow him. Peter's chains just fell to the ground. He passed the guards and the prison gate opened up all by itself and let him out.

When the angel left him, he made his way to a house where many people were praying for him.

He knocked at the door and a servant girl went to see who it was. She recognised Peter's voice, but didn't open the door. In her excitement, she rushed back to tell the others that Peter was outside, but they thought she was crazy! Peter had to do a good deal of knocking before they let him in.

God had answered their prayers by sending an angel down from heaven to set Peter free. And he can send an angel down to help us in our times of need too."

"Like a guardian angel?"

"That's right."

"That would be exciting. Have you seen an angel, dad?"

"Not that I'm aware of, but I do know when God is working in my life."

"How do you know?"

"When things work out in my favour or he helps me because there's nothing else I can do. But not all prayers are answered immediately. Sometimes it can take weeks, months or even years.

That's why people sometimes think that God isn't listening to them. But Jesus tells us to ask, seek and knock, which means we're to keep praying constantly. Like the parable of the widow woman in the Bible. She kept going to see a judge to get justice over her enemies. The judge kept saying no at first, but because she kept on pestering him, he decided to help her, as he was afraid she would wear him out!"

"So I'm to pester God?"

"Yes, if it's for something good and is really important to you," dad replied.

They joined the queue outside the school gate and everyone moved forward when it was opened.

"So I'll see you at one o'clock," dad said, after a quick kiss. "And don't forget to pray."

"I won't."

That afternoon, dad walked to the athletic ground for the school's sports day. He took a seat in one of the stands, next to the father of one of Mia's classmates.

"I can't believe the sun's come out," the man said.

"It's a real blessing," dad replied.

It took a while for him to spot Mia, with so many children on the field. She waved back in response to his call and got ready to run her first race, which was the hundred metres.

Dad was positioned to see the climax of the race and at the starting whistle, he hollered, "Come on, Mia," as she and several others powered up the track.

Mia got off to a good start, but she soon tired and was overtaken by two faster runners. Dad still cheered her on. He had to move to different parts of the stadium to watch Mia's other events and at three o'clock, when it finished, he went over to her teacher, so that she could be dismissed.

"Well done Mia. Let me take your bags."

"Thanks. I'm so thirsty," Mia said as she took a drink from her bottle of water as they left the grounds.

"You didn't need your rain mack after all," dad said.

"I prayed about the weather all morning and God answered me."

"Indeed he did."

"I'm going to pray about everything from now on."

"Including being a faster runner?" dad teased her.

"No. I only did it because someone else dropped out, but I had fun today and I'm really glad you could come this time."

"So am I."

"What are we having for dinner tonight?"

"I'm cooking."

"Mum will be pleased. What are we having?"

"What's your favourite?"

"Chicken curry. Is that what we're having?"

"Yes."

" Oh, goody. I've been praying about that too."

126

"There's no stopping you now is there?"

Mia simply laughed.

GRACE

"Dad, where's my present?" eight year old
Vinnie asked his father, who had stood up to leave.

Neil looked at Vinnie's mother, then his son.

"I'm a bit short this month, what with
Michelle expecting the baby and everything."

"But you promised," Vinnie cried.

"I know I did son and I'll make it up to you
next month." He ruffled Vinnie's hair. "Enjoy the
rest of your birthday and I'll see you all later."

"Your dad's skint," Jack teased, when the
front door had closed. He was Vinnie's younger
brother.

"Shut your face." Vinnie rushed Jack and wrestled him to the floor.

"Vinnie, Jack, stop all this fighting," mum commanded. She separated them and sent Jack upstairs.

"I know you're disappointed, Vinnie," mum said to him a bit later. "But there's no point in taking it out on your brother."

"He started it first."

"I know, but you're older and should know better. Your dad does love you, you know."

"No he doesn't. He only cares about his new family."

"At least he came to see you today. If he didn't care, he wouldn't have come, now would he?"

Vinnie didn't look convinced. He was deeply unhappy.

"It's not fair!" Vinnie shouted. "Jack's dad always buys him things."

"That's because he can afford to, and I always make sure that you share everything, don't I?" Vinnie's bottom lip started to tremble. "Come and sit down beside me." Mum patted the sofa. Vinnie plonked himself down and she cuddled him.

"I used to get upset about the things I couldn't control, Vinnie. But now that I know God, I don't let things get to me so much. I know it's hard at your age, but God can help you."

"How?"

"By his grace."

"What's grace?"

"It's God's goodness towards us."

"God's not good to me."

"That's just where you're wrong. He's very good to you and in lots of different ways."

"What ways?"

Just then, Jack crept back into the room and wanted to sit on mum's lap.

"Come on then, Jack, I'm just about to tell Vinnie how good God is to us."

130

"I want to hear. I want to hear," Jack said. "Can he give us some sweets?"

"He does give us sweets and chocolates and ice cream…"

"And bananas!" Jack hollered.

"That's right," mum continued. "He gives us all the wonderful food and drink we enjoy every day. Just think about *all* the different fruit and vegetables there are and *all* the different kinds of plants and flowers. Plus *all* the creatures in the sea and *all* the insects, birds, and animals."

"And gorillas," Jack said and started to mimic one.

"Thank you, Jack."

"What has any of this got to do with me?" Vinnie asked.

"He's given us so many good things to enjoy, but let's look at God's grace towards you, Vinnie. He watches over you and keeps you safe every single day. Remember the time you pulled a chest of drawers on top of you?"

131

"Oh, I remember that." Jack started laughing.

"I could hardly see you when I ran into the room, but you were completely unharmed. You didn't even get a bruise. And the time you fell down the stairs. You were laughing your head off at the bottom and weren't even scratched!"

"It happened so fast. One minute I was climbing over the balcony and the next thing I knew I was laying at the bottom," Vinnie recalled with amusement.

"It was a very dangerous thing to do, Vinnie, but God protected you. Not that it means we should go around behaving recklessly, because that would be testing God and he wouldn't like it. But it's worth bringing these things to mind. How else is God good to you, Vinnie? "

"Don't know," he shrugged his shoulders.

"What about your talent for playing football?"

"I love football."

"That's why you're in our local team."

"I'm good at riding my bike," Jack added.

"Yes, you are Jack. God is good to us even when we don't deserve it or are unkind to one other; like when you tease your brother. What do you think God wants you to say to Vinnie?"

"Sorry, Vinnie," Jack apologised.

"Forget it," Vinnie replied.

"God's grace is a free gift. We don't have to do anything to earn it and it doesn't have to be our birthday or Christmas or any other special occasion. He just likes to give us good things because we're his children and he loves us. I believe that the best gifts come from God. That's why he gave me you two."

"And he gave us *you,* mummy," Jack said.

"Yes, he did." She pecked his cheek. "I'm sure if you try hard enough, you can think of many other examples of God's grace towards you, Vinnie. I want you to think of some before you go to sleep tonight and just thank God for them. Do you think you can do that?"

"I'll write them down."

"That's a good idea, because then you'll have a constant reminder to make you feel better when you're feeling a bit low. I just want to say a prayer over you right now, if that's okay." Both children closed their eyes. "Dear Lord Jesus, help Vinnie to appreciate everything you have given us in the world to enjoy and the gifts and talents that you have given him. Let Vinnie remember all the times you have protected and helped him and let him know that you are always there, whatever is going on in his life. Remind him that all he has to do is call on you. I ask this in Jesus' name. Amen."

"Amen," said Vinnie.

"Amen," said Jack.

"Right," said mum. "I think it's time we got ready to go out for your birthday meal."

"Burger and chips!" Jack shouted.

"Pizza," said Vinnie. "That's what I want."

"Then that's what you shall have," mum stated, settling the matter.

TRIALS

"Why does God allow bad things to happen to people?" Karina asked aunt Jenny as they watched the lunchtime news about an earthquake.

"God isn't responsible for the bad things, Karina. It's the devil who wants to steal, kill and destroy."

"But isn't God supposed to be more powerful than the devil?"

"He is."

"Then why doesn't he save more people?"

"He does save lives; it's just that it's not always reported and we don't get to hear about all the miracles that happen. But we do hear about some miracles, like when someone is rescued after being trapped under rubble for days."

"But they've lost their family, home and everything."

"That's often true, but God gives them the strength to rebuild their lives. A disaster can bring people closer together and bring them closer to God. They make us realise that we're all in God's hands and depend on him for everything. That's why we shouldn't take anything for granted, because it can all be snatched away in an instant." As soon as Jenny uttered her last words she regretted it, for Karina's eyes started to redden.

"I didn't need to tell *you* that did I?" Jenny said by way of apology.

"It's all right," Karina said weakly, as tears spilt down her cheeks.

Jenny joined her niece on the sofa and gave her a hug.

"I miss her too."

"I just don't understand why God didn't save her."

"It's a question I've asked myself many times, Karina, but it doesn't get me anywhere. I've come to the conclusion that we cannot see the bigger picture, but God can and he knows what's best. What the devil meant for evil, God can turn to good."

"How?"

"Well, your mum isn't suffering anymore. She's with Jesus in heaven and is probably looking down on us right now. Do you think she wants to see you crying?" Karina shook her head. "Then let's show her how brave you are."

"I'm not feeling very brave at the moment."

"I have days like that too, but things will get better, I promise."

"How do you know?"

"I know because God is our comforter and he's working things out for us all the time; like you coming to live here with me. We have fun together, don't we?"

"We do, and I'm glad to be living here. I don't want you to think I'm not, but dad's still not very happy about it."

"Your dad hasn't been in your life for years and the court took into account what you wanted. He just doesn't see it that way."

"I don't like him being horrible to you."

"Neither do I, but as long as we girls stick together we'll be all right. I don't want you worrying about anything." Karina started to scratch her forearm. "You see, it's making your eczema flare up."

"I know."

"Jesus told us not to worry, because he knows what we need. We've got to live each day as it comes and pray about our problems."

"I pray for dad all the time."

"That's the best thing to do. You see we all have to face trials in life, Karina, some of us more

138

than others. But believe it or not, these things are sent to make us stronger, not weaker. They prepare us for the challenges ahead."

"In what way?"

"You know the story of David and Goliath, don't you?"

"Kind of."

"Well, you know that David killed Goliath with a catapult when no one else would fight him. What you might not remember is that David was a shepherd boy and his sheep were regularly being attacked by lions and bears. But David wasn't afraid of anything. He'd chase right after them, grab hold of them by the neck and kill them. I don't think I'd be in a hurry to chase a lion or a bear. Would you?"

"No way."

"Those animals didn't know who they were dealing with, did they?" Jenny said and Karina laughed. "Well neither did Goliath. He didn't know that David had faced great dangers before and succeeded with God's help and would succeed again. In the same way God is preparing you for something in your life."

"For what?"

"We don't know at the moment. We'll just have to wait and see. But I'm sure it'll be something that you or others will benefit from, because we can learn something from everything that happens to us as long as we stay positive. When we love God and trust in his promises, we know that he'll be with us through whatever we're facing. Our job is to remain faithful to the very end, and then we'll be an overcomer."

"What's an overcomer?"

"Someone who keeps believing in God's word however dark things get."

Just then the sound of scratching noises came from the back door.

"I'll go and let him in." Karina jumped up and ran from the room.

Rio, the Border collie, bustled in, swiftly followed by Karina, who knelt down and buried her face in the dog's musty fur.

"Can I take Rio for a walk?"

"As long as Tanya goes with you," Jenny said. "Where is she anyway?"

"Upstairs, probably," Karina replied.

"No I'm not," Jenny's daughter said on entering the lounge. Tanya aged ten, was two years older than her cousin.

"Do you fancy taking Rio for a walk with me?" Karina asked her.

"I was going to ask mum if we could go to the shops anyway. I'll go and get his lead."

As the two girls walked down the street with Rio straining at the leash, they chatted about school and their friends. It had been an overcast day, but the sun broke through the clouds and Karina felt an overwhelming sense of peace in her spirit. She had many things to be thankful to God for and being able to live with her favourite aunt and cousin was one of them.

THANKSGIVING

"Let's go to the Rec and have a kick about," dad suggested to Tyler, who was watching TV.

"I don't want to," Tyler replied moodily.

"Why not?"

"I'm watching TV."

"You need some fresh air and so do I, so go and get your trainers on."

"I don't want to play football, dad."

"I hope you're not still moping about that match. Because if you are, you need to get over it."

Tyler played football in a junior club on Saturday mornings. Yesterday they had played against another club and family and friends had been invited to watch.

They put him in goal, which proved disastrous, as the score was three nil. Some of the other team members taunted him as he came off the pitch. Even his own team mates gave him the cold shoulder, which made him feel even worse. He had no idea why he had played so badly, especially in front of his dad. Not that dad had been unkind. He said that professional footballers had to deal with the highs and lows of the game and he was no different. But it still bothered him.

"I hate football. I'm rubbish at it."

"That's not true. You just had an off day. We all have them. It's very easy to be negative and focus on what's gone wrong, instead of remembering all the things that have gone right; and believe me *that* list is a lot longer."

"But people always pick out the things I do wrong. My teachers are worse than anyone. They *never* let me forget."

"It doesn't necessarily get any better when you're an adult. Some people are just mean, but others are kind and encouraging. I could let my boss get me down, but I'm not going to give him the satisfaction. Do you know what I do when I'm feeling sorry for myself and hard done by?"

"Tell me."

"I think about all the good things in my life."

"What good things?"

"All the good things God has given me."

"What has he given you?"

"Your mum, you and your sisters for a start."

"But we're not rich or anything."

"No, but we're comfortable enough. We've got a roof over our heads and have plenty of food to eat."

"Most people have got that!"

"But not all. Especially in other parts of the world."

"You can have those things and still be unhappy."

145

"Yes, I know, but imagine how much harder it would be if you or any of us was sick? It's important to give God thanks for our health too, because it can change at any time and shouldn't be taken for granted."

"I am thankful for that, dad, but I'm not happy about the way God made me. He should have made me smarter."

"I hear you, Tyler. I wish I was taller and better looking, but I can't change that. God made me the way he wanted me and he made you the way he wanted you. Perhaps if you work really hard and pray to God, you'll get smarter, but maybe not in the way you expect. There are different types of intelligence and God will guide you to what he wants you to do with your life."

"I don't like letting you and mum down."

Dad joined Tyler on the sofa and put an arm around him. "It's not us you need to worry about letting down, Tyler. God will be the final judge. He will judge whether you've used what he's given you for the benefit of yourself and others. He'll judge whether or not you followed his commandments and he'll judge whether you've been thankful for all that he's given you. Being cheerful and positive is a sure sign of thankfulness, because then we have hope for a better future, however bad things look in the present. Okay?"

"Okay, dad."

"And we need to be especially thankful that God didn't leave us in darkness, but chose us to be his children. Being a Christian means that we believe that Jesus is the son of God, that he came to earth and died on the cross and took upon himself the sins of the world. This means that when we die we'll be with Jesus in heaven. That's something to be thankful for, isn't it?"

"Heaven will be brilliant."

"It will, but we want to put that off for as long as possible. Let's be thankful that we still have the freedom to worship him in this country without fear. In some places Christians risk their lives just to hear the Bible being taught."

"That's terrible."

"Have you heard of Thanksgiving day?"

"I've seen it in films."

"In places like the United States of America, they celebrate Thanksgiving every November, and they are giving thanks to God. We should be doing that every day of our lives because there are so many things for us to be thankful for."

"I'll start from today," Tyler said and smiled.

"That's better. Keep smiling and don't let anything or anyone steal your joy."

"I won't. I'll go and get my trainers on."

"Good boy. I love you, Tyler."

"I love you too, dad."

"I'll go and pump up the ball."

It was cold and breezy as they walked the short distance to the Recreation Ground and apart from a few dog walkers, it was very quiet. More